M000032720

RAIN
REVOLUTIONS

Rain Revolutions

Bessie Flores Zaldívar

Long Day Press
Chicago

ISBN 9781950987177

Library of Congress Control Number: 2020946883

Cover Art by Andrea Aranda
instagram.com/andrea_aranda

Layout by Joshua Bohnsack

Printed in the United States of America
First Edition

Para mi abuela Tesla y mi abuelo Cesar

Gracias por cada mañana que me dieron desayuno acompañado de historias

Solo el pueblo salva al pueblo.

y gracias ma' por haberme parido aquí
—Bad Bunny

Contents

Foreword

Ayendy Bonifacio

Bessie Flores Zaldívar writes, "the sky roars like a chorus of hungry bellies. Any minute now, it will pour down." It is powerful poetic lines like this that throughout *Rain Revolutions* illuminate the lives of people fed up with their circumstances and ready to come down on their oppressors like a downpour. Zaldívar's *Rain Revolutions* delivers un aguacero of vivid imagery, metaphors, and scenes that illustrates the complex lives of Catrachxs in Honduras's capital city, Tegucigalpa, fighting for themselves and their country.

Catering to readers' senses, this chapbook transfers us to the streets and homes of Tegucigalpa where we encounter the sounds of traffic, the smells of rotting mango and strong cologne, and the touch of lovers in the heat of love. It is a world full of poetry where Zaldívar's characters teach us that "everyone has a right to their own scars," the scars of love, motherhood, marriage, and, perhaps most important, the scars of our birth nations.

Electrifying and heartfelt, sensually captivating, and real, these beautifully written stories take us through a city dressed in vendors, lovers, revolutionaries, taxi drivers, and mothers, where graffitied walls speak against corruption, and the streets pulsate with stories of love and loss, life and death, and war and insurrection. This is a place where truths bend for freedom, and freedom means justice.

The characters, uniquely distinctive, are at war with the corruptible parts of themselves and their country; they wage war on debased politicians, invaders, and each other to be a little freer. Zaldívar's strong women characters lift a nation, hold characters together, and protect them from harm. In the case of "By This Time Tomorrow," a mother's love is a prayer in the form of advice: "Let someone else stand. I don't want to have to collect your body parts."

Rain Revolutions is a book about soft drizzles that turn to downpours. This is a literal and figurative lluvia that converts puddles to torrents washing over busied Tegucigalpa streets, over political murals calling for freedom and peace, and accumulate into apocalyptic floodwaters that deliver life and death to our posterity. After the stories' aguaceros, the ground hardens with truth and life, hope for better futures.

Zaldívar skillfully gives us a counter-narrative to American exceptionalism, where Honduras is the epistemic center and the shadow of the U.S. empire obscures the lives of Catrachxs like darkened heavy billows ready to deliver rainfall.

Rain Revolutions is a chapbook that I didn't know I needed until I read it. It is a magnificent text by a magnificent talent.

Lluvia sin Agua

Tegucigalpa, Honduras // 2019

"It doesn't matter that it rains," a man on the radio says, "if it's not raining in the right place."

His voice is familiar to everyone in the taxi: the older woman with acrylic nails almost as long as her fingers and as red as her lipstick, the man in tight dark jeans pulled down to his crotch, leaving his plaid boxers purposefully exposed, and Evelyn, sitting between them, with a green plastic basin on her lap. Whenever the car breaks, which is every few seconds, the mango seeds and skins inside the basin slide around, hitting the plastic walls around them and the large metal knife used to dismember them, and that now drips with the pulp of their transformation.

Evelyn wants to bury her face inside the tub. She doesn't care for the smell of mango, no. Not after three years of selling sliced mango verde with salt and pepper at almost every stoplight in Tegucigalpa. But the smell of the man's cologne is giving her one of those headaches that feel like there's a balloon behind her eyes that keeps inflating, its rubber skin turning thin and translucent, but never popping. If her abuela Chayo was here, she'd say he's wearing 7 Machos, "Y el ultimo estaba muerto." And the last of the machos was dead.

All the windows are already down. It is rare to find a car in Tegucigalpa that drives with its windows closed—except at stoplights, where everyone quickly rolls them up in time to avoid people like Evelyn, trying to sell or ask for something.

"¿Todo bién, flaca?" the driver asks, looking at her through the rearview mirror.

She's known Dario for years. They live in the same barrio. He plays fútbol with her brother. Most mornings, Dario gives them a ride to the city and, sometimes, he also brings them back. During these rides he mostly talks to Enrique about politics and soccer. She just listens. Occasionally, she catches him looking at her through the rearview mirror.

He is one of three taxistas she trusts enough to ride with even after sundown, even with other random passengers inside. If they were to get mugged by a marero posing as a passenger, she believes Dario would protect her. He would give them his money without a remark, and ask them to leave them alone, firmly. But if he was by himself, he could fight back, Evelyn thinks. He is a strong man with big hands and thick, hairy fingers.

"Todo bién," she says, locking eyes briefly. His reflection is sliced in half by the wooden rosary hanging from the mirror, perpetually swaying back and forth.

"Well, if you're going to vomit, make sure to aim inside that paila. No water to clean that backseat, you know," he says, winking.

She knows. Everyone in the country knows. She suspects the water shortage is the reason the man next to her decided to bathe in cologne instead of water and the traffic is slower than usual. Everyone in the area is rushing home. There was a rumor that today at five the camion-cisterna would return to their barrio. The big truck that sells water to the areas outside of the city that don't have a water system. Ever since the water shortage began, the trucks came to el barrio less and less, until eventually it was just once a week. They figured they could sell their water at a higher price to those with more money in the city.

"Dario, the time?" Evelyn says. She hasn't cleaned in a week. She stinks like old sweat and dried period blood and mango pulp.

"Four forty-seven," says the older woman, rolling her eyes. Evelyn notices she doesn't have any hairs on her eyebrows; instead, light-brown eyeliner arches over her eyes. On the middle of the left line, there's a small hairy mole—the only hair over her eyes.

"We won't make it. Walking would be faster."

Evelyn agrees. She's considered it a hundred times. Any other day, she would walk. But outside, the sky roars like a chorus of hungry bellies. Any minute now, it will pour down. She doesn't mind getting wet, but the lightning terrifies her. In the last few days, she has spied on the cover pages pasted on newspaper stands at least three mentions of someone getting struck. She knew someone from her barrio who died this way, two years ago. A boy, 16 or 17, who used to fix A.C. units with his father in the city. He was blasted into pieces. His father had to mop bits of his guts and brain from the walls of the rich people's house. That's what she heard.

Evelyn thinks of when she gets home, to the room she shares with her brother. Maybe he's there now, maybe he has been able to buy some water from the truck, or get leftovers for free. Sometimes they get lucky like that. But she doubts it. Enrique is also a peddler in Tegus, but instead of mango, he sells plastic electric mosquito zappers. He, too, gets the product from a man in their barrio that lets them keep twenty-percent of what they sell. They go zap-zap whenever anything hits the net. If she's close enough when Enrique plays with them, the hair on her arms stands. She hates them. They remind her of the lighting.

She doubts he's made it home. They try to hit different stoplights and parks, in case a particular area is slow, the other can make up for it. This has been their survival model for three years now, ever since she turned 16. Enrique has been a seller even longer. He used to come with their mom to the city before she passed, maybe since he was nine or ten. He's months away from turning 27 now.

If she's not misremembering, he is even farther away from home today than her. If neither makes it home on time, they won't have water for a week. They'll stink even more. She already has to hold her breath whenever Enrique walks by, which in a one-room space, is all the time.

"I'm walking," announces the man next to her. "Tenga," he says to Dario, handing him a crumpled bill of 50 lempiras.

"Me too," says the old woman, paying her own fare. "¿You going anywhere near Los Pinos, mijo?"

They slam their doors and sprint across the street. Evelyn realizes she's been holding her breath. Slowly, she allows her nostrils to relax and her body to take up more space of the sunbaked leather backseat.

"With them gone I can have you home in five or seven, flaca," Dario says, holding her gaze through the mirror, "but you're not gonna make me look like one of those fancy ass drivers all alone in the front. Get over here."

The smell of the cheap cologne isn't as strong in the front. Dario's scent, car grease and deodorant that has been sweated through, overpowers it. The car moves a few meters, putting them right in front of a broken stoplight that blinks all three colors on and off. Looking at it too long, she feels the balloon behind her face expand.

"This one never works," Dario says. "Nothing works en este país de mierda."

In its place, a traffic officer in a yellow vest blows his whistle and points to cars, deciding who gets to go when. Cars honk from all sides of the street. Some do in beats, pa-pa, and some hold their note, paaaaa. Cars try to go and brake and try to go again and brake again. The traffic of Tegucigalpa is a poem about near misses. To Evelyn, it feels like her balloon has grown strings, five thousand of them, and they're all being pulled from different sides.

"You look sick," Dario says. "Do you still have any mango?"

"Nothing," she says, "Besides, you ate two bags already."

Dario clicks his tongue and puts his arms behind his head. The traffic officer waves them over, and he pushes his foot on the pedall, keeping the steering wheel straight with his knee.

"You know I love eating your mango, flaca."

She blushes and says nothing. He does this from time to time, says things that can mean other things. Gives her free rides. Buys more mango bags than anyone really eats. She likes seeing his big fingers struggles to get the thin mango slices out of the tight plastic bag. The truth is, she has wondered before if he has a woman or any lost children. She imagines he must have some child. Most men do.

The men on the radio keep talking about how it can rain for days, but if it's not where the dams are, the water shortage will continue.

Then they move on to the president, and the water fountain he is inaugurating this Thursday in front of the church in parque central. A symbol of hope.

Stuck in another long line of cars, she knows they won't be home anytime soon, but in case she has any doubt, the sky opens and drops all the water the country doesn't have on them. Dario keeps saying, "Ya va pasar, ya va pasar," as if willing it, but the rain doesn't pass. The taxi's windshield wipers haven't worked in years. In seconds, they can't see anything, only rain falling on rain falling on rain. Even the back lights of the car in front of them disappear. Evelyn has never been underwater, but she imagines this is what it must look like. Dario has, once, when his cousins dared him to swim in el Rio Choluteca, the brown, murky, disgusting river that bisects Tegucigalpa, where the poor shit and the poorer bathe. He didn't open his eyes.

"¡Puta!" he says, pulling over, blindly, leaning over the open window to see. "¡Puta, puta, puta!" His black thick hair is drenched, drops sliding down, holding on to the tips as if terrified to fall. They park next to a gray-brick wall with the words FUERA JOH in blue spray paint. It would be hard to find a wall that is not vandalized with demands for the current president to quit.

"We'll wait it out," she says, "let's just wait."

"I'm sorry," he says, rolling up his window, locking all the doors.

"Meh, this is how it is. Just change the station, please," she says, "if I have to hear about water or Juan Orlando one more time, I swear."

"I know, I know," he says, turning the radio dial to the right and the volume one to the left. He settles on a song she has heard before, the kind of song in which all the people in it say their names and countries at the end. A new Reggeaton bop. It doesn't help the headache, but she prefers it to the men and their talk.

"You can lean the chair back if you want," he says, "the lever is on the side. Just pull up."

She does. They can hear voices and honks and thunder and yelling, but it's all muffled by the rain and Bad Bunny. They have never been alone like this, in a small space with nowhere to escape. Now a thick sheet of water conceals them from the rest of the world. He leans back too and turns on his side to face her. She becomes more aware of her stink, and tries to hold her arms as close to her body as possible.

"You think your brother made it home?

Where was he today?" he asks.

"Maybe, I don't know. I hope so. I hope he gets us water, if the trucks come."

"They won't. They can't with the rain. All the major streets will be flooded by now. Maybe tomorrow."

She says nothing, because there's nothing to say. This is just how it is. She looks at him instead. He has the longest eyelashes she has ever seen. Not that she goes around noticing people's eyelashes.

"He's a good man, your brother. Takes care of you. Protective. Probably jealous."

"We're not like that," she says. She wants to add, you don't know us. But she doesn't. She's bothered by his statement, but she can't tell why.

"What are you like, then?"

"He doesn't mess with my business and I don't mess with his."

"What kind of business do you have?"

"None. Not like that. Not like what you mean. Look, if Enrique wants to get his dick wet, that's his problem. And my business, is none of yours."

"Okay, okay, flaca" he says, "disculpá. No te queria ofender."

They stay quiet for a while, glancing at each

other from time to time. And then, without thinking it, she says, "Do you have a woman?" And he's surprised, so surprised it takes him a beat to respond, but then he's firm. "No, I don't. No woman, no kids."

She doesn't say anything, and after a few more beats, marked by the rain on the roof, he puts the tip of his index finger on her knee. He slides it down to her calf, and back up to her thigh. And then he puts his whole hand on her, and she's not surprised by how heavy it is, heavier that any hand should be. And she loves it. His hand travels away from her leg, to her abdomen, to her arms, to her face, back to her abdomen, over her breasts. She knows where this is going, and she wants it.

But she thinks about her stink and her long armpit hair and how she got her blood two days ago and it passed fast but they haven't had any water to clean their clothes or themselves and she doesn't want it anymore, not right now. So she stops him.

"I thought you wanted it."

"Another time," she says, "Not in the taxi, on the street, in the middle of a storm."

He believes her, even if none of those reasons are stuff she cares about.

They wait a few more minutes, in silence,

and then the rain has slowed enough for them to try to get to el barrio. An hour later, he's dropping her off, and says he can give her a ride to the city tomorrow morning if she's ready at 4 in the morning.

Enrique isn't home. For a minute, she thinks about asking Dario in. The thought makes her throb. But the reasons why she stopped him in the taxi are still there, and she knows inside are all of their dirty clothes spread around. The tub they use for shit and pee might still be dirty; she can't remember cleaning it out, and Enrique rarely does.

But she wants this. She has wanted this for some time. Quickly, she makes some calculations in her head. When will the water trucks come. When will Enrique be at the spots farthest from home, staying late in the city. When will she have time to clean and cut her armpit and leg hair.

"Dario," she calls. He has already started the taxi.

"¿Si?"

"El Jueves. En la plaza."

"What?"

"El Jueves, that's when. That's later."

It takes him a second to understand. Then his eyes open wide and he smiles without showing his teeth and nods.

"Ok, flaca. El Jueves."

The trucks don't come on Tuesday or Wednesday. They just don't come at all.

She wakes up at three in the morning to get ready to go to the city, per usual, but there's nothing to get ready with. Enrique brought two bolsas con agua home last night, but it's drinking water. She feels her dry throat and imagines it a few hours from now, when she's under the sun. Her eyes squinting, sweat pooling under her breasts and sliding in individual cold drops from her armpits to her waist. The thought of using her drinking water to clean makes her thirstier.

But then there's Dario. She pictures him with his elbow resting on the driver's window and his right hand on the wheel. What kind of woman would she be if she broke her first promise? She hasn't seen him since Monday. Enrique found them a ride that left earlier for both days. He hasn't been around her usual spots, which isn't weird, necessarily, just sad. But today they will meet. The mayor of the capital and the president are inaugurating a fountain at the Iglesia los Dolores, downtown.

Hundreds of street sellers will be there. The taxistas will try to give rides to people attending the ceremony. The park will be full. They'll leave together and come to her house. Enrique will be out, out until midnight, at least.

The basin where Evelyn cuts her mango is lined with pulp that has hardened into a crust in the past two weeks. Some of it has begun to grow a white and gray sponge-like shell. The knife is sticky. The smell of rotten mango is similar to that of a child's vomit. It overpowers other odors in the room. Their noses have become accustomed though, so she's only taken back by it when it has been several hours since she last smelled it. Enrique sleeps. He'll be up in the next twenty minutes or so, but right now his snores are steady and loud, contrasting of the soft rooster song outside. The room is dark. It's still at least two hours before the sun rises. Their eyes have also gotten use to this.

Evelyn takes off her shirt. Pained, she rips a corner of the water bag with her teeth, spitting out a bit of plastic that swished into her mouth. The hole is small, as small as she could make it in order to control the water spring coming out of it. She takes the smallest of gulps and then pours some over her right armpit. She takes the knife, and with her left hand pulls an assemblage of her armpit hair as straight as she can and cuts. They're long enough to curl and coil. She has used the knife for this before, but has had water to clean it after. She cuts as much of it as she can, and then does her other armpit, and then her legs, and then she finds she can't stop, and she cuts some of her pubic hair too. By the time she's done, all the water is gone, and her sticky knife is full of dark, thick, curled body hair.

Evelyn tries to wipe it with her shirt and a rag. It's not ideal, it's not what she wanted, but she feels ready. She feels like she can be with Dario like this. She knows she still smells, but much less. And she's not hairy. And she's a woman, and he is a kind man with long fingers and heavy hands.

She gets dressed. Enrique wakes up, gets fresh mangos and more mosquito zappers from Don Rafael, and finds them a ride with Don Julio, another taxista. An hour later they're in the city.

"I'll be by the stadium until noon, and then I think I'll move to el Bulevar Morazán," he says. "Good luck at the park. I heard Juan Robando would be there. Be careful with the police." That's what Enrique always calls him, robando instead of Orlando. Stealing. Juan

Stealing.

"Si, Kike," she says, "I'm riding back with Dario."

And with that he leaves, carrying his T-shaped pole with the hanging zappers that dangle with each of his steps.

Evelyn makes her way to the park and finds a spot under a palm tree. As usual, el centro is flooded with people trying to sell or buy something. She likes this area of the city. During the day, it's alive with peddlers and a few tourists. The streets are narrow, too narrow for three cars to drive besides each other. Every structure is old, but she can tell that unlike the rest of the city, downtown wasn't a random buildup of structure upon structure. The churches and museums are all painted the same peach color, and all other buildings sport similar graffiti. Stencils of the faces of people who have been murdered or dissappeared, messages against the government, insults against politicians, a random declaration of love. BERTA VIVE. FUERA JOH. POLICIAS ASESINOS. TE AMO LUCIA.

"Cacahuates, cacahuates a diez," a woman nearby calls. Another one sells bananas and plantains. Men sell fútbol t-shirts, zappers, phone cords, pirated movies with pixelated images printed on them. It smells like feet and fried food. A bachata song plays through low-quality speakers. She starts to peel and chop her mango, slithering slices in the small, see-through plastic bags. She keeps the salt and pepper in even smaller plastic bags with holes in a corner, so she can pour a little over the mango before selling it.

The ceremony is about to begin. Hundreds of black and gray pigeons with greenish-purple necks hang around the church, eating whatever has been dropped and then flying to the church's windows and bell towers. Stray dogs sleep under the shadow of trees, scratching and turning, flapping flies away with their tails.

There's no new fountain. Not the kind she expected, anyway. Not a ceramic structure with a fish or bird or other small animal spitting water over delicately carved flowers and designs. Instead, there are holes on the ground, twelve of them, with metallic rings over each. Together, the holes form a semi-circle. She knows water will shoot up from them when the president or the mayor get here and cut the gigantic ribbon.

In minutes the plaza floods with TV reporters. Men carry heavy, long cameras on their shoulders and women smile at them, holding microphones to their chest.

A few tents have been set up with long tables inside to sell merchandise. The sellers working them are different from Evelyn and her brother and others that, like her, are selling out of a basin or a bag. Those are government-sponsored sellers. They sell jam in glass bottles and hand-made jewelry. Their products sport stickers with the flag, all five starts. Evelyn's mango does not.

La plaza gets more and more crowded. Military police walks around. Six of them accompany a man who gets out of a black car. He's the president. She has seen his face on newspaper stands and graffiti enough times to know it. He walks slow, shaking people's hands, smiling to cameras. Evelyn knows many people hate him, but she can't really say why. He's a bad person, that's what Enrique says all the time. He is involved in drug dealing. It seems to her that that's what they say about everyone all the time, though. He's a narco. He's cousins or brothers of a narco. He is friends with narcos. He is married to a narco. All the same.

A girl and a boy approach her. "Cuanto la bolsita?" they say. She sells them for 10 lempiras each bag. They take three. She puts the money in the canal between her breasts.

She's not yelling mango, mango, mango a diez like she usually does. Today she can't concentrate on selling. And she doesn't want to sweat. She keeps scanning the plaza for Dario. She imagines him leaning against his taxi with his hands in his pockets, watching all of this. She wants to find him and leave as soon as possible. For one day, she does not want to think about selling. She can do that tomorrow. But she can't find him. He's not standing with the other taxistas by the left corner of the park.

Juan Orlando makes his way to the middle of the semi-circle fountain. It's easy to follow him because of the bulk of people and police around him. There's a woman who stands by him the whole time, holding his hand every so often. Evelyn figures it must be the first lady. He answers questions, holds microphones, points his finger to a camera, punctuates his words with hand gestures, laughs. After a while, people retreat from the half-circle, and it's only the president and his wife in the middle. The water jets are turned on. Big, thick springs fly through the air, taller than the president, and then curve down in acute angles. He laughs, and his wife laughs, and then they're out of the semi-circle, drying with towels, talking to more people, answering more questions.

A kid that has been standing by Evelyn, asking for money with a McDonald's cup full of coins, runs to the water. The coins clink inside as he moves. He lifts his shirt and stretches it over the spray, so that the water goes in from below his shirt and comes out over his neckline. More kids join him. Soon, all the waterjets are taken by children and a few adults.

Evelyn spaces out staring at the scene. She wonders if the water is clean, clean enough to bathe. Maybe she can find a cup or bottle in the trash and fill it up. She's looking for a trashcan nearby and doesn't notice when men in military gear and black boots start surrounding her. The flashlight of a camera hurts her eyes, making everything purple and white for a minute. It's loud, and someone is shoving a foam-sponge gigantic microphone to her face.

"Si, si... el presidente Hernandez loves mango! He's buying some right now from a woman in la plaza central, ladies and gentleman," a voice says.

"Presidente Hernandez, a man of the people! Buying some mango verde from una vendedora ambulante!" says another. "The president used to have his own mango tree when he lived in Lempira as a child. He spent many afternoons reading under it."

He's right there, in front of her, stretching his hand. It strikes her how normal he looks. He's not wearing a suit or a tie, just a white button-down shirt tucked in and jeans. He smells good, not like the man in the taxi on Monday or Dario. His cologne is strong and clean.

"Señorita," he says, "how much for a bag of manguito verde with salt and pepper?"

There are so many faces staring at her. They all wait for her to speak.

"Ah… eh…" she mumbles, "es…"

"It's okay," he says, "tenga."

He hands her a 500 lempiras bill. She has never touched one before. The bill is so crisp, that for a moment, she thinks it might be fake.

"I don't have enough mango or change for this," she says.

"No, no," he says, "just one bag. Just one bag of manguito verde, porfavor. Keep the change"

She gets a bag and adds the salt and pepper right there. The light is still blinding her. Her movements feel slow and clumsy. The president has a hand on her shoulder and is smiling so wide, she can see all of his teeth. His hands are cold, but much lighter than Dario's. Once she's done prepping it, she hands him his mango.

"Mil gracias, señorita, mil gracias."

She hopes he walks away right then. He doesn't. He starts eating the mango in front of her, his delicate fingers fishing into the bag.

"¿Quiere?" he asks her, offering a slice. She declines with her head.

He licks his fingers after each slice. That's when Evelyn sees it: two small but thick curled hairs stuck to his lower lip. He licks the area around his mouth, the hairs disappearing with it. And Evelyn can't stop staring. There's another by his cheek, and some in his fingers.

The cameras are all on him and her. She's sure they can see it too, but no one says anything. She expects someone to slap the bag out of his hand or whisper something in his ear. Nothing happens. Finally, when he's done, someone hands him a wet towel. He wipes his hands and shakes hers again. They all walk away. Evelyn stares at their backs, convinced one will turn around, arrest her or something. She can't move.

But then he is there. Dario, emerging through the retrieving crowd, smiling.

"You sold mango to the president?" he says, laughing. "You're gonna be on TV, flaca!"

"Shut up," she says, shaking her head and slapping his arm playfully. "Let's get out of here."

"Let's," he says, reaching for her basin and knife.

Maybe it's the concoction of smells of downtown Tegucigalpa in that moment, or the raw sensation in her hands of the fresh mango flesh she just cut for the president, a man who couldn't feel hairs on his tongue, or the echoing of faraway thunder over the children's laughs and the springs' splash. It doesn't matter that it rains, if it's not raining in the wrong place.

"No, no," she says, "leave it."

"¿Que?" he says, still holding on to it. "¿Segura?"

"Leave it."

He wrinkles his face but does as he's told. The knife clanks against the concrete floor and the paila topples over.

"Vamonos," she says, stretching her hand. "¡Apurate!"

And he's so moved by her rush, by her need of him, that he doesn't care about the basin or the knife or the stupid mango or an explanation or tomorrow.

"Vamos," he says, taking her hand. She runs, leading him through the water springs, to their waterless neighborhood, where they'll make an ocean out of a mattress. Quench a thirst, ache with another.

By This Time Tomorrow

Two countries in the world
have burnt their American embassy.

Tegucigalpa, Honduras // Abril 1988

You can't burn the American embassy if you plan it too much or too little. Too much, word gets out—those gringos have ears everywhere. Too little, they fuck you up or you fuck it up.

Mom is in the kitchen listening to her tiny old radio when we get home. She's praying along with a famous local father but turns down the volume when she sees us.

"I was beginning to get worried, muchachos," she says. "What have I told you? Try to call ahead if you're going to be after ten, por favor, que les cuesta, I get so nervous, no entiendo que—"

Roberto cuts her off with a hug, and she rests her head on his chest. "Perdón, jefa. We lost track of time. But we're here." He kisses her forehead, and she melts into him. This is how they've always been with each other.

"Diana is staying the night," I say.

"Si, si, of course. Dianita is always welcome. ¿Como has estado mijita? How's your mom?"

"Bien, bien, Doña Maria. Thank you for

letting me stay," Diana says, leaning in to let Mom kiss her cheek.

Mom begins her interrogation on where we've been and how it went (late-study group for Diana and me, long shift for Roberto at La Bola de Oro, the textiles shop where he works after classes). We say nothing about the Frente Estudiantil Hondureño (FEH) meeting where we were actually at, or the embassy, or tomorrow. Our mother is a strong woman: moved to Tegucigalpa from La Lima young, left her parents and younger sister behind. She raised Roberto and me all by herself working any odd job she could find. She's a tough woman—the kind with calloused feet and vein maps tattooed on her legs to show it. But she can't stand any talk about protesting or revolutions.

"I was listening to that program you all like earlier, the one in which they let anyone call in without even verifying if the things they say are true. One of you must've left that station on. Ustedes saben que I don't like it. But I heard this woman call in, talk about how they found the body parts of her son spread all over the carretera that goes to Santa Lucia. A torso, a head. He had been missing for a week. She says they dyed his hair blond so she wouldn't recognize his corpse. They had to use his teeth to identify him. Tan horrible," she says, crossing herself, "Dios bendito. This is why I don't like you out late or hanging out with in those students fronts."

"I heard about that too," Roberto says. He's putting away dishes, drying them first with a rag made out of an old school uniform shirt. "But that's why the student fronts are important, Mamí. They push against the military state and the death squads. Against American control of the country. Against the literal kidnapping of our citizens. If we don't stand—"

"¡Ya, ya, ya! Let's not start with that again, Roberto Miguel. Let someone else stand. I don't want to have to collect your body parts. No mother should have to do that. All this revolution talks and things stay the same in this country. Different people, el mismo cuento. Lo sabre yo, with my father en La Lima and his protest. ¡What it cost us!"

"Mamá, all Roberto is saying is that—"

"¡Ya, dije!"

Roberto and I reach the usual verdict with one glace. Let it go. Tensions about los desaparecidos, the opposition, and the government have been boiling hot and stirring fast for the past two days. Not just in our house, but the whole country. On Tuesday, Matta-Ballesteros, a local drug-lord, was kidnapped during his morning run by American authorities. He was taken to Dominican Republic, and from there formally extradited to the U.S. Matta might've been a criminal, but that didn't make him a villain. Not to us. He helped anyone with unpayable medical bills who came by. He built schools and hospitals. On Sundays, a line of people waiting to be served a free breakfast forms outside his house, circles the block like a cluster of ants around a breadcrumb. And if we're talking legal, his capture isn't. Honduras has no extradition deal with the U.S. Mom liked Matta too, but the second he got arrested and the protests began she was all about the war on drugs. Can't imagine how she'll feel about it all tomorrow.

Roberto keeps drying dishes and Diana helps him put them away. After a while the tension slips off our shoulders like dead hair and Mom resumes telling us more chisme about her day. Whose daughter is pregnant and whose man was spotted outside the motel two streets down, that kind of thing. It's all laughs if we don't tickle the country-shaped wound she carries on her tongue. Finally, we all kiss her and say goodnight, but she stays behind finishing her prayers. I hear her go on about the woman from the radio before closing my bedroom door.

In bed, I turn on my side, facing the wall, away from Diana. She undresses at the other side of the room—four feet away. Her belt buckle clinks against the floor and her bra strap snaps lightly against her skin. There's unzipping and pulling of fabric, stitching extended to its limits and infinite elastic threads stretching around her body, then relaxing again by the time they rest around her feet. I hear her brush her teeth and the faucet running. She turns the light off and I feel her weight on the bed seconds later.

We haven't said a word to each other since we left the kitchen. Or the meeting. The air feels heavy. Thick like Mamí's masa de tortilla tomorrow morning. It's just how it's been between us recently. Not all the time, but a lot of the time. Friends for ten years but this new boyfriend, Raul, is something else.

"You don't fall asleep that fast," she says.

"I wasn't pretending to be asleep."

"Mhmm."

"I don't think any of us will be sleeping

tonight," I say, still facing the wall, "not unless we drank enough for it, like your boyfriend."

"So, quarter till four, right? And the group at the south entrance of the embassy will make sure there's—"

"You know all of it already. We don't need to go over it. I'm sure Raul has reviewed it with you a million times."

I turn to lay on my back to be able to see her from the corner of my eye. She chose one of Roberto's old Olimpia soccer jerseys to sleep in. I keep a pile of those in the back of my closet for her and me. They're oversized for us, of course, so it gives the illusion that's all she's wearing. Her hairy arm and bare leg brushing on my own borders feel charged, like pressing your palm against a TV screen. A soft drizzle strokes the roof. I stare at the dark spot in the ceiling lined with yellow rims, like grease on a napkin. New ones appear every time it rains. We fill the house with basins and cups and plates to catch it all. Mom hates them so much. I know they're not pretty, but they're the ceilings own scars. And everyone has a right to their scars.

"He said he loved me, you know," she whispers.

"Raul?"

"Mhm. He said if anything went wrong

tomorrow, he wanted me to know that. I said I loved him back, but it's like he didn't believe me. He said he knew I wasn't there yet, and that that was okay with him. Someday soon. He is always so sure of everything—where to eat, best way to burn the embassy, our future children's names."

"Yeah?"

She sighs and turns on her side to face me. I close my eyes and turn to face her too.

"Rosa, by this time tomorrow we will have shown them. Los gringos pendejos will know they can't just come here and take our people illegally and expect us to take it."

Tomorrow

Roberto, Diana, two other FEH members and I take the bus from la UNAH to the National Soccer Stadium; from there, a taxi drops us off near the embassy. One of the guys carries our group backpack full of empty glass bottles and strips of fabric inside. Every time the taxi breaks or turns they clink. It is barely audible under the radio, but it feels like the loudest touch in the world.

A crowd of protestors surrounds the building when we get there. They hold signs demanding Matta's return. An older woman holds one that reads, "Patria SI, Gringos NO," with color-pencil drawings of bleeding bananas. People throw rocks, sticks, and bags of gasoline at the front gates. "¡Fuera Gringos!" "¡Fuego, Fuego!" "¡Regresen a Matta!" Several windows on the first two floors are already shattered. Spider-web cracks stretch like the roots of a Ficus tree. Every time a pair of blue eyes bites into a banana the glass breaks a new cut, Ficus-root thick.

The crowd keeps getting bigger. It takes a while to reach the Esso gas station by the northern gates in the midst of con permisos. Roberto goes inside the market-store and gets a Milo chocolate drink for him and two Fantas for Diana and me. More people we recognize from FEH and other student fronts gather nearby. One of the guys from the taxi checks his watch every few seconds. Then finally he signals to cover our mouths with the bandanas.

Four men begin to take cars from the customers unlucky to be here at the wrong time. We go inside and get the plastic gasoline bottles from the store. The cashier yells a couple times, but it's clear he won't interfere. He stares for a couple seconds, and then jumps over the counter and begins to help. "A la mierda con estos gringos," he says. "My dad was disappeared a year ago. They won't even tell us where to find his body."

We get the empty glass bottles from our backpack to assemble Molotovs. I'm not done with my first when the stink of burning tires and fabric is already gashing my nostrils. Screams and small explosions slash the air from all directions. Our hands move fast but clumsy, bumping against each other. The front entrance of the embassy where people line for hours every morning to go in for interviews catches fire first.

One moment I'm passing something to Diana and the next Roberto is pulling us. "¡Come on," he says, "let's go! The guards are running out through the south entrance. There's shots coming from inside. ¡Vamonos!"

He's shouting right in my face but sounds far away. Diana won't stop coughing.

"What?" she yells. Roberto begins to repeat himself but decides to pull us instead, and we begin to run after him.

The smoke is so dense I try to part it with my hands, like swimming breaststroke. Even with vinegar-wetted bandanas pressed to our mouths and noses, my eyes burn and the inside of my mouth tastes like half-chewed aspirin.

From the corner of my eye I catch sight of a boy—Roger, I believe his name is—burning an American flag in front of the main gates. A man with a camera takes a picture of him. There are half-burned American flags everywhere—some with burnt stripes, others with burnt stars. The smoke plays tricks on my eyes—I see the red, white, and blue melt from the flags margins and protestors' hands and fall into the streets like rivers of melted crayons. In the asphalt color puddles of wax harden into small hills. Then they break under our weight into shards of nothingness. The world is black and white except for the color explosions of melted flags—melted, not burnt.

People throw more rocks and sticks and Molotovs. The acidic smell climbs my nasal pathways, pushes against my forehead. We sprint, push, pull, and slither through the sea of limbs and sweat. Roberto holds my wrist so tight I can already feel the blood amassing at the surface to form a bruise. I hold Diana twice as hard.

We're barely out—reaching the tortillería at the end of the block, when we run into Raul. His nose is bloodied and his jeans browned, like he kneeled in dirt. He signals for us to follow him with his hands and realizes we can't hear him. Roberto begins to head his way but I pull him back.

"¡No no no! That way turns uphill. They'll get us. We need to head para el Centro, it will be easier to hide."

Roberto nods, but I'm not sure he can hear me. There's no time to make decisions. Raul keeps waving his hands. We run the opposite way. He catches up to us and pulls Diana's arm.

"¡Diana!" he yells, "Diana, come with me. We need to—I know where to go."

Diana looks back at me like she wants me to make a decision for her or go with her or something. I lean in and whisper-scream in her hear, "I'm not going that way," and let go of her hand.

We washed all the dishes twice. It's been two hours at least. Outside, the sound of footsteps, screams, shots, sirens, and voices has quieted. Our heart beats haven't.

"I think they're gone," the owner of the cantina says, coming into the kitchen. We don't know his name, but he let us come in when he saw us running from the soldiers. We knocked on every door.

The place is called Tito Aguacate. I remember seeing a story about it in a newspaper once. I have never been, but I know it's famous for being around since the '30s and for some drink with a weird name every ambassador who comes to the country tries. Above it is the owner's apartment. The old man told us to pretend to be dish washers, the three of us— Roberto, Diana, me. To clean ourselves first and then get washing, in case any soldiers came in. None did.

"A stay-in-place order has been issued," he says. He's so thin I can see the bones of his collar and ribs lining his button-down shirt. "You need to stay here tonight. I can give you something to sleep in and something of my wife's for the ladies," he says to Roberto. He only addresses him when he speaks.

"Do you have a telephone we can use? We need to let our mother know," Roberto says.

The man tells him there's one upstairs and leaves to get us clothes.

"I'm going to tell her we're staying at one of my classmate's house. That she doesn't know him. That we ran into him trying to get home, when the curfew was ordered," Roberto says.

Diana and I stay in the kitchen. She hasn't said much since we left Raul near the embassy. He wouldn't follow. She wouldn't leave us.

"It's going to be okay. We'll go home in

the morning. I'm sure you can call your parents from here if you want."

"They think I'm staying at your house. They won't be worried," she says, brushing her fingers through her hair. We look nothing like we did this morning when we left the house. But none of us are hurt, which feels like a miracle of its own.

"I'm sure Raul made it," I say. "He had a plan."

"It's not that," she says. "I mean—I'm worried about him, but also just tired. That went nothing like I thought it would. But I don't know what I thought. There were so many shots."

"I know," I say, "but we did it. You saw it burn. It caught fire so fast."

"That's what scares me," she says, "Don't you think everything happened too fast? That they seemed unresponsive at first?"

"They weren't expecting us," I say. "It was the surprise element."

"Maybe," she says. "I don't know. This could change everything, not in the way we thought. Things could get worse. They could get more aggressive."

"But it could also—"

"I just want to feel safe."

We can hear Roberto talking to mom upstairs, raising his voice, asking her to calm down.

Diana begins to say something and then stops, and begins again. "Listen. I want to talk to you. I've been thinking about Raul and—and how we're all getting older. My mom already had me at my age. Yours already had both of you. And I know, I know it feels fast and maybe sudden but our lives aren't going to be student front meetings forever. I want to feel safe and—"

I listen to her, nodding, chewing on the walls of my mouth that still taste like aspirin. Losing sight of the colors of the walls of this bar that smells like stale cigarettes. Feeling the walls between Diana and me form in my stomach.

Curfew is lifted and we make it home two days later. Mom hugs us in the midst of insults and prayers and scolding. Roberto lifts her and she stops crying to yell at him to put her down. Inside the house, the radio is turned up as loud as it goes. There's constant new reportages about the fire. Twenty-five cars burnt, no personnel from the embassy hurt. Five protestors dead from shots fired from inside the embassy. The whole protest took over two hours. Different politicians and military personnel are asked to comment on the consequences it will have for the country. It's the narcos, one says, they want to take control of the country. Now more than ever, we need to stand with our American allies and protect our freedom.

"¿Y Dianita?" Mom says.

"She went home."

"Hay, que pesar, but I can just imagine how worried her parents were. They called here every few hours."

"You should call Diana to make sure she made it home okay," Roberto says.

He switches the state to the one by the opposition party, the one mom hates. People are calling in to ask missing loved ones to get in touch if they can, warning that soldiers have begun to hunt anyone they believe involved using the photos taken by journalists to identify suspects.

It rings so many times I think she won't pick up, but she does right when I'm about to hang up.

"I knew it was you or Roberto," she says.

"So you're okay. Did anything happen on the way there?"

"There were a lot of soldiers coming inside

51

the buses, asking to see our IDs and addresses."

"Did you give them yours?"

"I had no choice. I couldn't think of a fake one fast enough. And I think he would've known I was lying."

"And Raul?"

"He's safe. He might try to come over tomorrow if his dad gets a circulating permit."

"Then by this time tomorrow you might be engaged."

"I have to go. I'm glad you're both safe. I'll call you."

Yesterday

"Rosa, by this time tomorrow we will have shown them. Los gringos pendejos will know they can't just come here and take our people illegally and expect us to take it," she says.

The soft drizzle has turned into a steady tap. I can't help laughing whenever she curses, it's so rare. She's one of those people that go out of their way to not curse. "Yeah we will, Dianita." She smiles and even though it's kind of dark, I see some shadows and reflections gliding on her teeth. Our noses touch. I'm not surprised by how cold the tip of hers feels. Ten

52

years and some things just are. "Your boyfriend doesn't know everything, you know."

She exhales in a way that makes me feel like I could trace that breath all the way to her guts with just a finger. "No. He doesn't. You're right."

She puts her leg on mine and I let my hand go to her thigh, run the tip of my fingers up and down her skin.

"Tell me more about how by this time tomorrow we'll have made history."

"By this time tomorrow," she says, "we'll be right here, in this bed. Celebrating."

"I think we can celebrate right now," I say, reaching for her, slipping my hand under the old shirt.

"I think we can."

United We Can

Based on the flooding of 1954
and protests against the United Fruit Co.

La Lima, Cortés, Honduras // 1954

They agree, unspokenly, to not worry until the water has reached the second wooden step. Tuesday at noon it isn't quite there yet, but when the wind picks up and builds waves, some of the brown murky splatters fly all the way up to Isaias's feet on the fifth—and final—wooden plank.

Upon feeling the cold drops, he flexes his long toes inward, like curled worms in the heat. Any other day, he wouldn't be able to stand barefoot outside the house, not even on the cool wood, much less without a hat. The sun is unforgiving in La Lima, as the white spots on his face and tan lines on his arms testify. But the sun hasn't been out since Sunday afternoon, when a soft drizzle quickly turned into a storm. A storm, una tormenta. How appropriate the name is—tormenta. It has been a torment.

He has told his two little ones, again and again, that one can get used to anything with enough time. But even days later, the violent spatter against the tin roof hasn't become white noise. This is what living inside a drum would be like, he thinks. Whenever it does stop for a few moments, the whistling of the wind chimes in. The strength is such that the tops of palm trees reach the ground when their trunks bend. It reminds Isaias of the women on the plantation: spines arched over their baskets and their long, thick hair escaping bandanas and hair nets.

They had known it would rain, of course. It was that time of the year, and the smell of moist earth had been hanging in the air for days. But they weren't expecting a flood.

"Papá, el agua," Josesito calls from the door.

For a moment, Isaias thinks he means the flood, the rain, all the water surrounding and covering them—he has learned in the last few days, trapped inside, that children have a habit of pointing out the obvious—but then he hears the whistling of the kettle, rivaling the whoosh of the wind. He follows the boy back inside, glancing one last time at the water level. First step and a half.

Isaias removes the kettle from the gas burner and pours the boiling water into the green plastic paila. The edges of the basin are peeled and scratched. He can't remember if it was the old dog, Tango, who chewed it or Josesito, when his teeth were coming in. The scraped plastic bits scratch his palms as he lifts it and carries it to the bed, but he barely notices. He grabs the last clean rag—he knows it is clean because he washed it himself. But no one else would be able to tell, not with its dirty-gray discolor and yellowish stains. It was birthed from an old shirt. He submerges the rag, squeezing and wringing it out, over and over. Finally, he places it on Eva's forehead.

"You're feeling trapped, Viejo," she says.

Viejo. He is eleven years older, not the biggest age difference he has heard of, but she chose "old man" as his term of endearment when she was seventeen and he was twenty-eight, and stuck with it seven years and two—almost three—children later. She keeps her eyes closed, which Isaias is grateful for. It's easier to lie this way.

"Just worried about the water rising. It might reach the second step by nightfall," he says.

"Mmm," she hums, "for the best. If you're all trapped in your houses, you can't be out there protesting. Less of a chance of getting killed. For all they know, you've had a change of heart and can't wait to get back to work, but the rain just won't let you."

"No one has a change of heart after fifty-seven days," Isaias says, sweeping the warm wet rag over her thighs.

"Hungry people do."

He doesn't respond, but continues to wash her legs, her belly, her arms, stopping every few seconds to wet the rag. Half of the time he can't tell whether she's kidding about the protest. But he understands, of course. Josesito has needed new shoes for weeks. Maria is looking even smaller than the average three-year-old. They both stink. They haven't washed in a couple of days; neither has he. All of the water has been used for cooking and keeping Eva clean and comfortable. They ate the last of the stinky gray bananas a couple of days ago. And the new little one will be out any day now. Any minute.

Isaias pushes down that thought, not for the first time today. It just can't be. How much bad luck can one family have? If the new one comes today, or tomorrow, there will be no way for Lupita, the midwife, to get here. And this is why they need the protests, right? They need roads with drains. They need hospitals outside the plantations. They need working conditions that don't involve him working sixteen hours a day, every day, and still not being able to provide for his family.

"Papá," Maria says, materializing next to him, tugging on his pants. "We're hungry."

Josesito stands a couple of steps behind. He has a habit of sending Maria when he wants something. He seems to think she has more sway with him, or is less likely to be ignored. Isaias is tougher on him, but not unkind, not unloving. Once, Eva accused him of liking the girl better because she looked like him so much.

"Ya voy," he says. "Go with your brother. See what can we make."

They scurry away, and seconds later he hears the pantry doors creaking open, slamming shut.

"Ya no hay nada," Eva says, opening her eyes.

"There's some rice," he says, almost sure. Almost. "Some coconut bread too." They can eat around the mold.

He leaves the warm rag on her forehead, and she closes her eyes again. He will need to hand wash more rags soon, but the bar of Lagarto soap is no longer a bar at all, but a thin, triangle-shaped slice that slips between his fingers. He knows he shouldn't have used brand soap at all; he should've sold it. It was one of the last things he got from the plantation's commissary before the strike began. The plantation officers wouldn't have found out that he sold the product, he thinks—not with the strike going on. But he couldn't remember how to make jabón de pelota anymore, ball soap. He remembers there is pig fat and ashes involved, that it has to be boiled and stirred for hours until it foams, that the whole house will stink for days. But he has forgotten the rest, and there's not enough gas for it, anyway. So he used the brand soap.

"We're going to need more clean towels when the baby comes," Eva says, as if reading his mind.

He takes her hand in his and glances at the cloth banner neatly folded on a chair near the door. It hasn't been used yet, so at the very least, it's not dirty. But it's canvas cloth, scratchy and rough. If he were to unfold it, the banner would extend nine feet wide and twelve feet long. In black bold letters it reads:

VIVA LA HUELGA, SIGAMOS ADELANTE, UNIDOS PODEMOS
                    – SECTOR 16.

Long live the strike. Let's go forward. United we can.

He could cut the cloth with Eva's fabric scissors, create small rectangles that will soften through wetting. He's supposed to bring the banner to today's strike, but maybe there won't be a strike at all. Not with the rain like this.

"We'll be ready when it gets here. We always are," he says.

It's true. He's been there for all of their children's births. When Josesito came, a December morning, the midwife had been there since the night before. And Maria was born in the plantation's hospital; he was already working for la United Fruit Co. then. It was all free. That was the year he got promoted as the Sector 16 chief, so they called her Maria Esperanza because she was all the hope he felt.

"Go," Eva says, "Go feed them."

He kisses her on the chin, nose, and forehead before standing. The baby will be here before the week's end, he's sure. But he hopes they still have at least a couple of days to figure out a plan. He will go to the protest today, and he'll ask Pedro or Ivan for some money. He has never been one to borrow, but his pride is worthless if he can't provide for his family. He'll get tortillas and rice, and they'll eat rice for lunch and tortillas with salt for dinner.

"Viejo," Eva calls as he stands from her

side, "we need to move the bed."

"Is there a gotera?" he asks, looking up. He hasn't noticed any dripping.

"No, I told you," she says, "the bed can't be facing the door. It invites death in."

He half sighs and half smiles. He's heard this before somewhere he can't place, just as he can't recall the reasoning behind it.

"Tell me why again."

She rolls her eyes. She knows he doesn't believe in all that stuff. He was raised in San Pedro Sula, the big city of the north. He hardly entertains his wife's beliefs. "Creencias de pueblo," he calls them. Village beliefs.

"You know why," she says. "That's how they take dead people out of the church, feet first. The bed can't be facing the door."

"We'll do it tonight," he promises, turning away.

"Papi," Maria says as he walks into the kitchen. "This." She holds up a small, yellowish cloth bag with the word arroz written in black marker in Eva's handwriting. The bag folds in on itself, on its emptiness. All of its contents cram in a corner.

It's a quick cook. He doesn't have to look for a pot or water. The only one they own sits on the burner, and all the water they have left is in the kettle, still warmish. He feeds Maria himself as she sits on his lap, stealing small bits from her plate every so often. Josesito sits next to them, barely taking a breath between mouthfuls. Rice grains stick around his mouth and nose. There isn't enough for Isaias himself, but he is able to make a decent plate for Eva. They eat in silence, too absorbed in the bland rice to talk. Even the rain has stopped.

"Josesito," Isaias says, once his son has licked the plate two times, "Do you know where your mamí keeps her big scissors?"

Josesito nods and gets up to get them from a basket full of threads and needles next to Eva's bed.

"Okay," Isaias says, feeding the very last grains to the girl, "I need to head out. I'll be back in a couple of hours. Josesito, make sure you keep washing your mother's arms and legs and belly with the hot towel. I'll bring food for tonight."

"Pero Papí," Josesito says, "el agua?"

"It's okay," he says, "it's only like this for a couple of blocks. It won't be like that on the main roads. They've got drains there."

"Papí," Josesito says again, "you think you could bring minimos today?"

"I'll try."

Both children love bananas. Everyone on the coast calls them minimos. It's the bananas they get for free from the plantation, those that are no good for export—the gray, battered, squelchy. The ones that don't meet the minimum requirements, los minimos.

Before climbing down the stairs, he folds the cuffs of his pants up to his knees. The water is dark brown. He considers taking off his shoes but knows there can be anything lurking beneath the water, anything that doesn't float. What does float and spreads all over the water's surface: watermelon rinds, plastic bottles, pigeon feathers and shit, cigarette butts, the wrappers of local plantain chips and yucca brands. What might not: broken glass, rocks, and other sharp objects.

He plunges his right foot. The water rises halfway up his shin. He feels the leather-like insole of his shoes sticking to the bottom of his feet. Only Eva could ever clean these shoes and make them wearable again after this, but she'll probably need soap for it.

Isaias walks through the water for several minutes, making big exaggerated steps, careful not to plunge his feet into the water too violently or too fast, to avoid splashing his clothes. He passes others, mostly men, doing the same. Children stand and sit at the tops of stairs, looking on at their fathers making their way through a sea of brown, parting shit and trash out of their way. He reaches a main road. He is right—those are not flooded, but his shoes now are. He tries to dry them by flapping them in the air for several seconds.

He walks toward the meeting point, la Plaza Central, around the Francisco Morazán statue. It is a huge iron monument of the man riding a horse that's reared up on its back legs. It has been highly vandalized in the past few weeks. White letters exclaim different messages around it now: United Fruit asesinos, Viva el Trabajador, Justicia, Green-go, Gringo.

A few blocks before he reaches the plaza, Isaias runs into other protestors. Like him, their pants are folded to their knees and barefoot, dripping shoes in hand. Pedro sees him and walks over to shake his hand, extending the gesture into a half hug.

"Listo, jefe?" he says.

The men from Sector 16 started calling him boss after he was named Sector Chief. They chose him as the protest leader for their sector too.

"Ready," Isaias replies. "Hopefully the rain didn't discourage the people."

"It didn't, jefe," Pedro says, shaking his head. "La gente knows this is important. We have to be out here rain or shine if we want them to take us seriously."

"Asi es," Isaias says.

"You got the banner, jefe?"

"¡Mierda!" Isaias says, grabbing his forehead with one hand. "I forgot."

"That's alright. It's probably for the best. It could've gotten ruined with the water."

The plaza vibrates with men and women carrying banners and flags. Isaias makes his way to the stairs surrounding the statue, with Pedro following close behind. Other sector leaders are already there, carrying their own banners. He feels guilt bubble in his throat like ball soap, boiling and rancid. He doesn't want his sector to feel underrepresented.

"They're here," the Sector 12 leader, Juan, tells him when he reaches the top stair.

Isaias turns to see what he means. At the south of the park stands a wall of policías, at least fifty of them. Armed.

"They can't do anything if it's a peaceful protest," Isaias says. He knows better than that.

"We will march from here to the train tracks, then follow the tracks to town hall," Juan tells him.

Isaias nods. He knows. He was there when the march routes were decided.

"¡VIVA EL TRABAJADOR!" Juan yells to the crowd.

"¡LA HUELGA Y LA PATRIA!" they yell back.

They walk out of the park slowly, repeating the same words and phrases. Some of the men carry heavy banana bunches and hand them to those around. Isaias grabs a few whenever offered, thankful that he'll be able to bring them back for the children. He turns to look at the police before they leave the park. They remain unmoved. He's sure there are some waiting at the town hall already. So far there have been no protest-related deaths in la Lima. Nearby cities and towns have not been as fortunate. In El Progreso, there were six deaths, all protestors. In Tegucigalpa, there were at least a dozen, policemen and protestors.

He's grateful for the absence of sunlight now. The first few weeks of the protest were brutal. By the time he got home each day, his shirt was completely drenched with sweat. It was almost as if he had been working at the plantation all day.

He joins in on the chanting, determined to make up for the lack of banner with his spirit.

He's doing just that—chanting and raising his fists—when it happens. At first, he can't hear it. Not with the loudness around him. But then Pedro pulls on his shirt to make him turn around.

"¡ISAIAS!" a woman yells. "¡ISAIAS BARAHONA!"

It's a neighbor, one of Eva's friends. He can't place her name, but he has seen her at the house before, perhaps picking up clothes that Eva had fixed for her. She pulls him by the collar of his shirt. Her face is red and several strands of hair have escaped her once-tight bun.

"¡Isaias, the baby! ¡Eva is having it now! We could hear her screams all the way to the house. My husband is here. I had to come get you. Maria, your girl, she came out to the balcony and yelled, '¡Josesito! ¡Josesito! ¡Get papí!'"

She speaks fast. Isaias can barely understand her but gathers the important bit: the baby is here.

He starts to say something to Pedro, but Pedro quickly interrupts.

"¡Go!" he says. "¡Go, compa!"

Isaias runs. It took him twenty minutes to get here, but he can be home in ten. The woman follows closely behind for the first couple of minutes, but after a while, she falls back. He thinks he hears her yell that she will catch up, will get someone or something. When he reaches the shore of the flooded area, he doesn't stop to fold up the cuffs of his pants, which have unspooled since he started running. He wants to throw the bananas, leave them there, but he can't bring himself to do it, to disappoint the children. He places two between his chin and neck and tries to hold them there by pressing his face down. Indeed, sharp things do hide below the water surface. Something punctures his left heel, but he doesn't stop to look or feel.

Before he can even see the house, he hears her screams. And he can make out an accompanying cry: Maria's. The girl has a tendency to cry when others do. Isaias fights the murky water, moving his legs as fast as he can, desperate. The water fights back. It has begun to rain again, or maybe it has been raining for a few minutes now. He doesn't know. His vision is blurred by the falling droplets, and his body is trapped, the water now reaching his waist. He's only a few meters away when he decides to dive, to swim the distance. He thinks he will move faster this way but it proves impossible with the trash piling around him. With his whole body now wet and muddy, he stops after a few strokes and resumes the awkward water-walking. When he reaches the stairs he holds the side rails with both hands and pushes his feet to the third stair. He goes up two at time, slipping along the way, hurting himself, choosing not to feel.

The front door is open. He finds Eva not in bed but a few steps from the door. She is laying on the floor, screaming and crying. Around her, non-water liquid spreads. He can hear Maria's cries somewhere, too, but he doesn't see her. He throws the bananas on the floor and grabs Eva by her legs and neck and carries her to the bed. Even though he was there for the birth of their other two children, he doesn't know what to do. He knows there is a lot of crying, pushing, and sweat.

"¿Que hago? ¿Decime, que hago?" he says. What do I do? Tell me what to do.

"Tenés que cortar," she says. You must cut.

"Where?"

She gestures with her hands. She keeps screaming my baby and my boy and other things he can't make out. Isaias tries to calm her down. It was like this last time too. A bunch of babbling and half-phrases, a bunch of screaming and crying. He wants to tell Maria to shut up so he can focus on Eva, but he doesn't know where she is.

It feels like at least half an hour has passed, but it can't be that long. He hears steps outside, and shortly after the woman who came for him walks in with another two women. Isaias stands and moves away, knows it's time for him to step aside, to let them do their thing.

One of the women gets between Eva's legs, struggling to keep them apart. Eva shakes violently, screaming. The other woman asks him about wet towels. He runs to the table where he left the scissors and begins to cut through the protest banner. His hands tremble and his fingers are too thick for the scissor holes. Frantic, he begins to rip the fabric with his teeth. He makes small, large, medium squares—or shapes that resemble squares. When he has a handful, he brings them to the women.

"Your foot," one of them says.

He's been leaving a trail of blood around the house. Blood and mud. The woman hands him one of the fabric pieces he cut. He is about to refuse, but she cuts him off, telling him to use it to take out the glass.

Piercing out of his heel is a triangular shard of glass. It breaks the surface of his skin like the trash spread out in the water—half-there, half-hidden. Some of the glass is painted red with the beginning of a white stripe surrounding it. It's a Coca-Cola glass bottle piece. Isaias wraps the corner of the fabric around it and pulls it out.

"She's crowning," the woman between Eva's legs says.

Isaias steps back. He tries to get them everything they ask for, but most things they don't have—more water, clean towels, cotton. They manage, because they have to. It can't be more than ten or fifteen minutes later that he hears the baby's cries.

"It's a girl," the woman says.

She cuts the cord and gives it to the other woman to store. They will bury it later. When there's dry soil to bury with, when there's time to think about futures and traditions.

The woman carries the baby girl to Eva. She looks purple and blueish. Eva holds her and cries more and more. Isaias tries to hold them both. He's never missed the birth of any of his children—he never will. He's sure of it in this moment. This is what matters most to him.

"Ya esta," he says, "ya paso. It's over. It's over."

But Eva doesn't stop crying and shaking her head. He must've blocked it out before, but now he notices, again, that Maria hasn't stopped screaming either.

"My baby," Eva says again and again. "My poor baby."

"She's okay," he says, "she's here, she's okay."

"Jose," Eva says, "Jose. I'm so sorry."

Isaias doesn't understand. She never calls him by his second name.

"Shhh," he says, "ya paso."

It seems impossible that he would hear it, considering all of the screams and cries going on, but this is a new sound—a horrible shriek. It comes from one of the women who stepped out to get his daughter. His older daughter. Maria.

He runs outside. On the balcony the woman holds Maria pressed to her body. With her hands she covers the child's eyes, but her own eyes are fixed on a spot in the water surrounding the house.

A few feet away from the stairs Isaias climbed just minutes ago, a small round mass of hair floats. Around it, the hint of unmoving arms and legs, little limbs breaking the water's surface, like a Coca-Cola glass bottle shard fracturing skin.

Note

Roger mentioned on page 46 is referencing, Roger Samuel Gonzalez, a 24-year-old student protestor who was kidnapped by an American-sponsored, Honduran-military operated death squad before witnesses on April 19, 1988, at noon, while walking through the Central Park of Tegucigalpa. He was later tortured and murdered. The armed forces denied knowing his whereabouts or anything relating to his disappearance, and said they were in fact looking for him in relation to the burning of the American embassy on April 7, 1988. Roger had been photographed there.

Acknowledgements

A grateful acknowledgement is made to the editors of the following journals and spaces in which some of these stories originally appeared:

On the Seawall, *fresh.ink*, and *Best of the Net 2020* anthology: "Lluvia sin Agua"

F(r)iction: "United We Can"

Born in 1997 in Tegucigalpa, Honduras, **Bessie Flores Zaldívar** is an MFA Fiction candidate at Virginia Tech. Her work has appeared in *CRAFT*, *[PANK]*, *Foglifter*, *Palette Poetry*, among others, and has been selected for *Best of the Net* and nominated for *Best New Poets*.

More about Bessie can be found at bessiefzaldivar.org

New & Forthcoming Titles

How to Adjust to the Dark
Rebecca van Laer

Milkshake
Travis Dahlke

The Everys
Cody Lee

Whimsy
Shannon McLeod

Love Stories & Other Love Stories
Justin Brouckaert

LongDayPress.com **@LongDayPress**